A LADYBIRD 'EASY READING' BOOK

'WELL-LOVED TALES'

The Old Woman and her Pig

retold by
VERA SOUTHGATE, M.A., B.Com.

with illustrations by
ROBERT LUMLEY

Ladybird Books Loughborough

One day, an old woman was sweeping her kitchen floor, and she found a crooked sixpence.

"A crooked sixpence!" she said. "That means good luck. I wonder what I shall do with it?"

"I know what I'll do," said the old woman. "I'll go to market and buy a pig."

So off she went to market. There she was lucky, for she bought a pig for sixpence.

As the old woman was going home, she came to a stile.

The pig sat down and would not jump over the stile.

The old woman said to the pig,
"Pig! Pig! Jump over the stile,
or I shan't get home tonight."
But the pig would not jump over
the stile.

So the old woman went a little further along the road, to look for help.

Soon she came to a dog.
She said to the dog,
"Dog! Dog! Bite pig!
Pig won't jump over the stile,
and I shan't get home tonight."
But the dog would not bite the pig.

So the old woman went a little further along the road, to look for help.

Soon she came to a stick.
She said to the stick,
  " Stick! Stick! Beat dog!
  Dog won't bite pig,
  pig won't jump over the stile,
  and I shan't get home tonight."
But the stick would not beat the dog.

So the old woman went a little further along the road, to look for help.

Soon she came to a fire.
She said to the fire,
"Fire! Fire! Burn stick!
Stick won't beat dog,
dog won't bite pig,
pig won't jump over the stile,
and I shan't get home tonight."
But the fire would not burn the stick.

So the old woman went a little further along the road, to look for help.

Soon she came to some water. She said to the water,

"Water! Water! Quench fire!
Fire won't burn stick,
stick won't beat dog,
dog won't bite pig,
pig won't jump over the stile,
and I shan't get home tonight."

But the water would not put out the fire.

So the old woman went a little further along the road, to look for help.

Soon she came to a cow.
She said to the cow,

"Cow! Cow! Drink water!
Water won't quench fire,
fire won't burn stick,
stick won't beat dog,
dog won't bite pig,
pig won't jump over the stile,
and I shan't get home tonight."

But the cow would not drink the water.

So the old woman went a little further along the road, to look for help.

Soon she came to a butcher. She said to the butcher,

"Butcher! Butcher! Kill cow!
Cow won't drink water,
water won't quench fire,
fire won't burn stick,
stick won't beat dog,
dog won't bite pig,
pig won't jump over the stile,
and I shan't get home tonight."

But the butcher would not kill the cow.

So the old woman went a little further along the road, to look for help.

Soon she came to a rope. She said to the rope,

"Rope! Rope! Hit butcher!
Butcher won't kill cow,
cow won't drink water,
water won't quench fire,
fire won't burn stick,
stick won't beat dog,
dog won't bite pig,
pig won't jump over the stile,
and I shan't get home tonight."

But the rope would not hit the butcher.

So the old woman went a little further along the road, to look for help.

Soon she came to a rat. She said to the rat,

"Rat! Rat! Gnaw rope!
Rope won't hit butcher,
butcher won't kill cow,
cow won't drink water,
water won't quench fire,
fire won't burn stick,
stick won't beat dog,
dog won't bite pig,
pig won't jump over the stile,
and I shan't get home tonight."
But the rat would not gnaw the rope.

So the old woman went a little further along the road, to look for help.

Soon she came to a cat. She said to the cat,

"Cat! Cat! Kill rat!
Rat won't gnaw rope,
rope won't hit butcher,
butcher won't kill cow,
cow won't drink water,
water won't quench fire,
fire won't burn stick,
stick won't beat dog,
dog won't bite pig,
pig won't jump over the stile,
and I shan't get home tonight."

And the cat said to her, "If you will go over to that cow and bring me a bowl of milk, I will kill the rat."

So the old woman went to the cow and asked for some milk.

The cow said to her, "If you will go over to that haystack and bring me a handful of hay, I will give you some milk."

So the old woman went to the haystack, for a handful of hay, and brought it to the cow.

As soon as the cow had eaten some of the hay, she gave the old woman some milk.

Then the old woman took the milk to the cat.

As soon as the cat had lapped up the milk —

the cat began to kill the rat,

the rat began to gnaw the rope,

the rope began to hit the butcher,
the butcher began to kill the cow,

the cow began to drink the water,
the water began to quench the fire,

the fire began to burn the stick,
the stick began to beat the dog,

the dog began to bite the pig,
the pig jumped right over the stile,

and the old woman *did* get home
that night!